THE EPIC OF BAYAJIDDA: BOOK I

The Epic of Bayajidda: Book I

Rise of the Ancient One

HAMZA LAWAL

Legend of the Huskahs

CONTENTS

DEDICATION

This book is dedicated to the ancient Mega-Lake Chad and all lakes that dried up and probably need saving.

~ 1 ~

AD 629: SETTLEMENT OF BIRAM

Cold dry air whispered as it passed by an old clay hut. The mud walls of the hut made a soothing echo and a tiny lizard disappeared into a crack to shelter itself from the dusty wind. The tall trees lost even more leaves as the dry season continued to turn everything brown. Tired eyes with sleeping bags stared deep into the murky night. With great difficulty and a deep breath an arm stretched and grabbed a mug full of porridge. A few gulps followed and an eventual sigh of relief.

A tall built man emerged from the darkened hut and made for the stable where a white horse stood alone. "Hisan!" he yelled and the horse trotted toward him. Hisan was the man's beloved horse —an *arav* (desert) horse famed for their beauty and stamina.

"However does he do it?" wondered Nebu out loud. A loyal companion who was one of the soldiers who refused to stay behind in the city. "I don't know," replied a local caretaker who worked the grounds of the village. The tall built man then knelt down and picked some hay-lage from a mound on the ground and the white horse's lower jaw dropped, and his nostrils relaxed and widened in excitement.

"You haven't eaten all day. I apologise my friend," the man said and gently rubbed the horse's back.

"Abu Yazid. We are hungry too," chirped Nebu.

"My friends. I know we are all tired and hungry but there is nothing I can do for now," responded the tall built man, as he walked back to his small hut.

Disappointedly, Nebu and the caretaker groaned, as they looked at their friend returning to his hut. Nebu was the only soldier who had come that far west with the former military general.

"Please do not call me Abu Yazid. Whenever you say that, I miss my little boy, Yazid," added the tall built man, his voice echoing from the empty clay walls of the high ceiling-hut where he lay shirtless on the ground staring at the woodwork.

"I will call you Bayajidda then," responded Nebu with a smile on his face.

"Baya- what?"

"Well that is what the locals here have been referring to you since we got here three years ago," replied Nebu, shaking his head from side to side and clasping his hands together.

"Has it really been three years? It's high time we return and get my family out of there," replied Bayajidda.

"Oh, yeah now you are talking, Bayajidda!"

"Hey, easy there with that name. The people here are quite funny. Who comes up with something like that?"

"In the local language here, it means 'not in Jidda' or 'he is not with Jidda'."

"Hmm, interesting my friend Nebu. I think they mean I am not interested in their religion— Jidda. For in our old language of the North we say *jeddah* means grandmother or the old religion of the grandmothers. This is where the legend of the Queen of Sheba comes from. The Queen of Sabeans which are today the Habsha."

"Wow, Bayajidda, you are so clever. You could have been a scholar!"

"Indeed, Nebu but I'd rather pick up a sword and save people."

~ 2 ~

KITAB AL WAFA(T)

As the freshness of morning came, Bayajidda rode down the insular hill they had spent the night on. His companion Nebu followed closely behind. They bid the caretaker goodbye and continued their descent into unknown territory— the home of the Habe. "I shall call this settlement 'Eastern Town' or "East for Biram," declared Bayajidda.

"And why is that?" asked Nebu.

"Well, because of my son Yazid, of course. His mother Magira calls him Biram."

"Oh interesting, Bayajidda," replied Nebu.

The descent down the highest hill was pleasant but ever so often Nebu would stop riding his horse and groan under his breath due to hunger and thirst. Nebu also noticed that the caretaker of the small settlement had followed them. However, after they had been riding for about half an hour the caretaker stopped walking and sat on the ground, motionless. Concerned with his safety, Nebu dismounted his horse and yelled, "Are you okay?"

"Nutrition has come to him as I said it will come to you too," replied Bayajidda but Nebu was confused as to what was going on. He looked upon Bayajidda as if to say can you explain further? But Bayajidda gave him a dismissive gaze and shortly thereafter, Nebu's pockets were filled with dates and other fruits. "Wow, Bayajidda! I have received nutrition too, haha," rejoiced Nebu.

"Yes, I told you both to be patient. This is the work of the Great scroll of Kitab al Wafa(t)," responded Bayajidda. "What... Is that?" asked Nebu, with his mouth full of dates.

"It is an old cartouche belonging to the Habe people I found in the old hut. It causes small fruits to appear," replied Bayajidda.

"Wow, Bayajidda and you were able to figure it out? What aren't you telling me?"

"Nothing Nebu. I went to school to study these things. That's all."

~ 3 ~

MIRACLE AT HABE-LAND

At the foothills lay a town belonging to the Habe people. Saharan sands beclouded Bayajidda and his companion Nebu's visions. The thatched roofs of the town became even dirtier and the cold unforgiving dry winds of harmattan carrying with it sands from the north reddened the atmosphere. From a distance a long queue of traders and their caravans appeared as caterpillars. Faintly, a voice became audible giving directions to traders. "Keep going, keep going. This way to the city of Kano," the voice yelled on and on, pausing only to inhale the sandy air that lingered perpetually in the atmosphere.

Bayajidda groped through his pockets looking intently for something. His eyebrows churned and at the right-hand side of his head was a vein gorged with blood. "Nebu this isn't natural at all," he said. Nebu, whose lungs were full of dust and billowing smoke which rose higher and higher, nodded in agreement.

"What is going on here?" Bayajidda asked the yelling boy as they approached the walled city.

"Today is the celebration of our God, that is why you see all the traders here," replied the boy of not more than twelve years who then carried on yelling at the top of his lungs.

Bayajidda and his companion dismounted their horses and tied them at the entrance of the town and he finally found what he was looking for inside his pocket. "This is a magical stone!" declared Nebu with a huge smile. As usual, he was very proud of his companion Bayajidda. "No, it's not magical, Nebu. It is merely a reading stone. It helps me magnify the writings on the scroll," replied Bayajidda.

"The Kitab al Wafa(t)?"

"Yes, that's correct," replied Bayajidda, as he sat comfortably on the ground and unrolled the scroll from which he read, "Oh sky full of beauty, seize in your support of the soil which now appears suspended in your midst. Please sky with all your beauty, incubate the sands no more and give relief to the people of this town. For they have remained many moons with no rain and no fresh air."

Nebu looked up in disbelief and utter shock as the sky which hitherto appeared full of dust and smoke had cleared and rain clouds formed; instantly making the air more breathable. Within a short period of time intermittent showers followed and settled all the dust and sand.

The Habe people rejoiced and Bayajidda was invited to their administrative building where a chief introduced himself, "I am Ubangiri," he said and motioned for

Bayajidda to sit on a wooden stool. Bayajidda reclined the offer, "I am in a state of urgency," he replied.

"Please, explain further," ordered Ubangiri.

"Well, my wife and child are in captivity in the Kanem. I came here to work so that I may earn enough to recruit men who can help me in my quest."

"Kanem? You mean the Zaghawa Empire?"

"Yes, Kanem comes from the word *anem* in their Kanembu languages and means south. As the lands turned dry, they came South. Many of my army are still over there, under captivity. While some have betrayed me," replied Bayajidda.

"Ah, very interesting. I am afraid we cannot help you. No one is going with you. The Kanembu, Gorane, Teda and Zaghawa are very dangerous. They come here and raid for slaves, yearly," replied Ubangiri, the Habe Chief. He sank back down into his most comfortable chair and took his attention away from Bayajiddah and Nebu and his eyes fixated on the masquerade that had come to town. Nebu looked at Bayajidda with a dissatisfied look on his face. "Why won't you help?" he asked.

"I told you people before. We are grateful for the rain but we can't help you against the Saif Dynasty; the Empire of the Sword who hold suzerainty over us. I know them well. Our people the Habe used to live in Paha in an area north of Meroe but decline in livelihood led us to travel South to Njimi the capital of the Zaghawa or Kenembu. Still that area became too dry and we came here and left them behind, north of the Great Lake but even here, they come for us. So, I will not falter in my position. No, we will not help you."

"But...but—"

"That's enough Nebu, he said what he had to say," interjected Bayajidda.

~ 4 ~

A DIFFERENT APPROACH:
MĪMRŌ (HOMILY)

Cursed since he was a child, Bayajidda was used to disappointments but he always maintained a magnanimous smile on his face. One day, as he laboured outside under the blazing sun while making furniture, he reminded Nebu that, "It is not out of schadenfreude that they refused to help us."

"I know," replied Nebu, he groaned loudly, 'so much to do all the time and never enough time', he thought.

"Oh, don't worry about that, Nebu. Where there is a will there's always a way," responded Bayajidda as if he had read Nebu's mind. He then began to sing loudly.

"What are you singing?" asked Nebu.

"This is *mīmrō*," replied Bayajidda. "*Mīmrō* is a liturgical song. It is sung in my native language. A type of homily, you know," responded Bayajidda.

"Ah, in Syriac!"

"Yes, I'll translate it to the local language of the Habe people for the children who come here to help us."

Moments later, young children gathered around Bayajidda and sang together with him. He relished at the sight of the excited children which reminded him of a childhood he never had. While his mother died in childbirth, his father was always away on frivolous trips. So, Bayajidda was forced to live away from the comfort of his father's mansion. Away from the kingly verandahs, gardens and royal courts where he would have learned about law and governance. Instead, he had to grow up in a lowly quarter in the outskirts of town with a relative, where he taught himself farming, carpentry, and singing hymns.

It would remain that way until he was summoned to his father's deathbed to take over as the only son, but Bayajidda opted for abdication instead which had a punishment of excommunication. Bayajidda accepted the punishment with a bow and the crown passed to his sister — making the dynasty shake to its feet, dividing the nation into two; those who chose to remain and those who decided to follow Bayajidda to the semi-tropical lands, south of the Sahara. The latter constituted mostly military men but unfortunately many of them were forced to remain in the city of Njimi.

***

Days passed and not only the children learnt to sing homilies but even the adults. On one such day, Bayajidda opened his shop and began to sing and the chief of the Hadeija clan of the Habe, Ubangiri called Bayjidda and expressed his happiness. "I am glad you've made people happy in this town," said the chief.

"The pleasure is mine," responded Bayajidda.

"You have brought rain when our crops withered. You have brought laughter and happiness and uplifted despondency from our hearts. For this reason, I will point you in the right direction that you may save your family." Bayajidda's eyes moved away from the chief and landed on Nebu who was so joyous his legs couldn't support his weight, which ultimately made him collapse to embrace the soil. "You will help us with men and horses?" he asked but Chief Ubangiri's expression was as firm as ever before. With a straight face, he replied, "No. The Rumawa will."

"Huh?" Bayajidda suspired in disbelief. "Romans?" he asked.

"Indeed. There are Rumawa here in Habeland living together with us. Follow that young man," replied Chief Ubangiri pointing at a reddish skinned child with flowing hair. "I didn't think Romans were this far south," said Nebu. Bayajidda nodded in confirmation and grasped his horse's reins. "Leave your horse. It is not a long distance," added Ubangiri.

~ 5 ~

RUMAWA (ROMANS)

"Bayajidda, Bayajidda! He is here, he is here!" Roman kids gathered around Bayajidda and welcomed him to the Roman quarter of town. "I was told you were on your way. We've heard so much about you," said a strong looking man with a metal helmet and a worn-out leather armour around his waist. He extended his arm to shake Bayajidda as others like him gradually emerged from their huts. "Thank you. I am honoured," replied Bayajidda, shaking the man's hand. "I am Jan-Damusa. The lord of all hunters in this area. I am told you need help against the Kanembu!"

"Yes, that is correct. My wife and child are there. She is a princess of that land, imprisoned by her megalomaniacal father — a pathological egoist," said Bayajidda.

"Hmm I know what you mean. We have had problems with the Kanembu since we came here. They usually attack these lands for slaves and we have been waiting for someone who can help us attack them."

"But you are so few. Even if all of you and all the Habe came together, you wouldn't stand a chance against the Kanembu," said a concerned looking Nebu.

"Relax Nebu. Firstly, we are not going for war reasons. We are going on a rescue mission," replied Bayajidda. At which point Jan-Damusa, the lord of hunters glanced at Bayajidda in objection. "We are going for war and nothing less," he said.

"But you will lose. I've lived there for some time and I can tell you, their defenses are no joke," replied Bayajidda.

"What then do you propose?" asked Jan-Damusa. Bayajidda made for a nearby wooden stool on which he sat comfortably with his legs stretched. He reached into his robe and retrieved the Kitab al Wafa(t); a scroll written in Syriac. There, he read about secret passages. "According to some who have studied these lands. The Great Lake Zad (Chad) can be accessed from here through an underground stream. From there, we will arrive at the Lake and then pass through another underground stream which will take us straight to the Mai's (King) quarter."

"Huh, you propose a suicide mission? I would not do that even if I were paid with the *Hur* (grapes) of paradise," lashed out Jan-Damusa. He turned his back to Bayajidda and walked away to the rest of the Romans who appeared forlorn after hearing the exchange between their leader and Bayajidda.

"Do not do it for yourself. Do it for the children that see you as their father. Do it for all the hunters and do it for the women who are taken every year. Do it for the young men who are made to work and do it for the Habe who welcomed you, O foreigner to their land," implored Bayajidda and Jan- Damusa stopped in his tracks. For a moment he raised his left leg as if he was going to continue on his way but instead, he turned around. "Let's do it!" he said.

~ 6 ~

'SUBTERRANEO'

Within a very short period of time, the Rumawa learned from Bayajidda that only through patience can they travel the way he proposed. Over the course of days, they prepared day in and day out until one day Bayajidda declared "We will leave by daybreak!" The Rumawa rejoiced and packed all their weapons and food but Bayajidda left everything behind including his horse. On seeing that, Ubangiri, the chief of the Habe clan of Hadejia smiled, knowing that Bayajidda intended to return. "We shall go to the Komadugu River and then from there we shall take the canoes to the beautiful garden village of Yo and then from there we shall access the subterranean passage to the capital of the Kanenbu— which is Njimi."

Jan-Damusa who wore a leopard skin raised his sword and made a loud cry of war which was answered by a congregation of young men who were eager to do as Bayajidda commanded but Bayajidda looked at Nebu and said,

"I wonder why they are so excited." He then said, "Less excitement and more caution please!"

***

By afternoon, they arrived at the orchard settlement of Yo, where everyone ate to their heart's content and even packed extra fruits. Many even laid down for an afternoon siesta except for Bayajidda, not a slight sign of tiredness could be observed in him. His calm expression was only betrayed by the vein on the side of his head which often appeared whenever he was under stress. His attention was focused on saving his wife and child.

Not long after, Bayajidda led them to a cave where they found the subterranean entrance into an underground river which would lead them to the Kanembu capital of Njimi but not without unexplainable events. The river glistened merrily as it caught the light of the sun but as they assembled their canoes on the body of water, they noticed something strange. "Why is it so salty?" observed Jan-Damusa. "No one should drink this water," he advised his fellow hunters.

"This is where the waters of the Great Lake Zad (Chad) drain to. For that reason, these rivers are very salty, while the Lake Zad is not. I suggest you leave all your weapons and the canoes here. Otherwise, they'll be lost. No one will sink, so we will go as a group. I will tie myself with this rope and pass it over to you all," Instructed Bayajidda.

One by one, they followed Bayajidda into the river which flowed underground from the cave. The river was deep but as it flowed inside the cavern system, there was always enough headroom to breathe between the body of water and the encasing rock/ karst structure. Just as Bayajidda had said, they did not sink and all they had to do was let the water carry them on its course. After about thirty minutes, the cave broadened; opening up into an area with an underground lake. Hundreds of small streams trickled down into the lake — microlitre by microlitre, drying up the Great Lake Zad into the waters below.

~ 7 ~

THE TRICKSTER

The air was still but humid and a lingering smell of decay, mold, moss, clay and wet stone ruled the underground chamber. Far above, the river Komadugu continued on its course sending fresh water to the Great Lake Zad but down below, the Zad was drained into a red lake, tinged by Dunaliella salina — an algae. The red subterranean lake twinkled brightly while trapped air underneath thick algae gave the appearance of curdling or lumping akin to stagnant blood. Bayajidda set alight a torch and the cave came to life. lengthy shadows spread to the far reaches of the cave and the light of the torch revealed human skeletons littered on the floor — the bones of adventure seekers who had lost their lives in the cave.

Nebu's eyes widened in fear of what might lurk within but very soon his worst fears were placated, as a strange man seated awkwardly on a donkey emerged from a shadowy area.

"Make yourself known. Who are you?" asked

Bayajidda, as he shone his torch closer to the figure. The man broke out laughing. "I am Jufa, haha," he replied. "In search of a short cut, you found yourselves here, haven't we? Haha. There is no escape. There is no way out."

"Nonsense, of course there is a way out," replied Bayajidda. Jan-Damusa, the leader of the hunters, glanced at his crew to reassure them that they would definitely find a way out. "I entered this cave since the time of those who make mountains," said Jufa.

"How then, do you still live?" queried Jan-Damusa but the strange man simply laughed and gently carried on riding his donkey until he disappeared into another shadowy area. "We shall continue, this way," pointed Bayajidda.

"Continue into the lake? "asked Nebu.

"The lake is hyper-saline, no one will sink. It is shallow from here, but it will get deeper, so you must hold your breath for a short while."

They plunged into the shallow lake and very soon, Bayajidda, Nebu, Jan-Damusa and his crew made it out to the other side of the cave where they found another river which was flowing in the opposite direction. Instead of water being drained from the Great Lake Zad into the salty subterranean lake, this time the river flowed uphill with tremendous speed toward the Great Lake Zad. "Hurry, this is our way. This river will take us up!" Screamed Bayajidda.

"They will not make it. They will all drown and their bones will be deposited back from the other river. Back to the banks of the lake below, just like the skeletons you saw

over there," said Jufa, still merrily seated on his donkey.
"Wait a minute, how did he get here so fast?" asked Nebu.

"There is always another way," replied Jufa.

"What other way are you talking about?" Jan-Damusa
walked toward Jufa and grabbed his head by his forelock.
Jufa's donkey brayed loudly and Jufa shoved Jan-Damusa
away powerfully. He then reclined back on his donkey and
said, "Only Bayajiddda can hold his breath for that long.
The rest of you will drown."

"What is the other way?" asked Bayajidda.

"Drink from the Fountain of Youth and you can hold
your breath for up to thirty minutes and also have your
youth restored," replied Jufa, as he pointed at a thick
milky liquid that seeped out from a crevice on the wall of
the underground chamber.

"What's the catch?" asked Bayajidda.

"Haha, the taste of that liquid is so delicious that after
having a taste, you will no longer hunger for food, or anything else that humans crave. For that reason, I doubt you
will continue on your quest. Whatever that may be."

The Rumawa led by Jan-Damusa headed toward the al-
luring liquid while Bayajidda pulled Nebu away from the
thoughts of going anywhere near the Fountain of Youth.
Wrapping his large hand around Nebu's mouth and nose,
he jumped into the torrential-upward flowing river which
seemingly countered gravity.

"Alexander the Great is with us down here, you know,
hahaha." Jufa's voice could be heard trailing as they
jumped into the river.

~ 8 ~

THE SAU (GIANTS)

The night was still, bitterly cold and dark. The moon did not appear save for a lone star which twinkled for a while and then disappeared. Xeric plants were scattered across the muddy ground and further ahead, was a gaping hole on the ground. It was the hole which moments ago was filled with a strange water which flowed uphill like a volcanic eruption but as mysteriously as it flared up, it stopped completely. Bayajidda regained his consciousness only to find himself covered in dried mud which slowly flaked off as he stood on the muddy ground. He Loomed over the hole in search of his companion Nebu or anyone else that might have made it out alive but there was no one. Further across, came the distinct smell of barbecue and as Bayajidda let his sense of smell guide him, he soon stumbled upon a bonfire with gigantic people with strange circular heads.

The gigantic people were nocturnal and their sense of smell far exceeded that of ordinary people. "Over there! There is another one," one of the giants yelled after spotting Bayajidda in the distance. "Why didn't you see him sooner, you idiot?" replied another giant who quickly lurched toward Bayajidda. Sauntering in the marshy terrain Bayajidda kept on tripping, as he was weighed down by fatigue and darkness but he was still able to have a glimpse of his friend Nebu tied in a cage near the bonfire. Soon Bayajidda's worst fears came to mind. He grubbled through his pockets in search of the Kitab al Wafa(t) so that he may recite something worthy of buying him some advantage against the giants but he couldn't find the scroll anywhere. As he continued to struggle, the giant who was already a few metres away from Bayajidda observed him closely with an intense look on his face. "So? Catch him already. What are you waiting for?" Shouted the other giant who was still at the bonfire.

"This one is different. This one knows a few things," responded the giant and those were the last words Bayajidda heard before the darkness of the unconscious took over.

***

The light of the coming morning would force Bayaidda's eyes open to see Nebu seated and eating fruits. "What happened? Where are the giants?"

"They are not cannibals. They just wanted to keep me warm."

"Tied in a cage?"

"I kept trying to get away, I was scared. That's why they had to tie me. They'll return in a while," replied Nebu but

Bayajidda was still not quite settled. He stood up and went straight to the giant's cave. "Where are you?" he asked.

"We are here, while the rest of us are sleeping. We sleep during the day and wake up at night. Why do you disturb us?"

"I wanted to thank you for saving my friend." replied Bayajidda.

"Is this the strange one?" The giant reached back into the cave and asked, leaving Bayajidda standing alone by the mouth of the cave and a smaller giant emerged.

"I saw you yesterday," said the giant.

"As I did you," replied Bayajidda.

"I said you were different because there is something I think you can understand. Usually, people don't know its use," said the giant.

"What do you speak about?"

"Come with me," replied the giant, leading Bayajidda toward the shores of the Great Lake Zad. It was the first time Bayajidda became aware that they had actually made it to the Lake. He sighed in relief after seeing the lake and motioned for Nebu to follow suit.

~ 9 ~

THE HIDDEN WALLED CITY
OF NJIMI

"I know where you are going. You want to go across the lake to the city of Njimi for some reason," said the giant, while pointing at strange glyphs on a small rock.

"Yes, that is correct," replied Bayajidda.

"You won't be able to access the walled city at this time. Soldiers are everywhere, even at night. You'd need this," said the giant, pointing at one petroglyph.

"Why are you wasting our time with this nonsense?" complained Nebu.

"Do not chastise him, Nebu. At least he helped you last night," reprimanded Bayajidda. The giant sighed disappointedly and looked away at the far reaches of the Great Lake Zad.

"These are tribal identifications," he said softly. He looked intently at Bayajidda to make sure he was attentive and then continued, "You will see many tribes with distinct symbols. The symbol of the Kenembu is this one.

If you master it, you will speak their language and they will not be able to tell that you are a visitor."

Bayajidda followed the instructions of the giant and concentrated on the symbol. When the giant became satisfied with Bayajidda's efforts, he stood up swiftly, getting ready to go to the cave to sleep. "I knew you could do it. The moment I saw you. Ninety nine out of a hundred cannot master a single symbol," he said.

"But where did you get these from?" asked Nebu. "These are the 'Ka' symbols. The one your friend is now working on is the *Ka-nur,* which means 'light head', this one is called the *Ka-mai* meaning 'water head' and this one is called the *Ka-hareeq* which means 'fire head', you see," replied the giant. He stretched his long arms and yawned wearily. "Though the tribes no longer know the meaning of their symbols or the power that lies within each symbol nor even the ability to use the symbols. The symbols are gateways to the culture, — a shortcut," he added.

"A short cut indeed," repeated Nebu.

***

As night dawned Bayajidda mastered not only the Ka-nur symbol but also the Ka-mai and with that, the mysterious city gates of the elusive Njimi revealed themselves behind towering sand dunes. Just north of the northern frontier of the Great Lake Zad was a city nestled within an oasis fed by underground aquifers, some of which were artificially channeled from the nearby lake. It was a marvelous city, but Bayajidda and his companion Nebu were not there for sightseeing. Very soon, Bayajidda was greeted by the guards who opened the city gates. "A great Mai has arrived," they said.

"Hurry up, let the Mai know that another great Mai (king) is in our midst," they ordered.

"No! You will not let the Mai know. I am here for the Meiram (princess)," commanded Bayajidda. The guards stepped to the side, to their relegated positions while soldiers emerged, curious to find out what the excitement was about but even they became befuddled at the sight of another Mai who by their tradition must respect and follow his orders. Bayajidda spoke the language of the Kenembu fluently. Under the powerful influence of the Ka-nur symbol and the strong influences of Ka-Mai— the denizens of Njimi had no idea what hit them. For the Ka-Mai symbol had the power to make its user a king of the Kenembu.

~ 10 ~

MEIRAM (PRINCESS)

Bayajidda walked confidently into the royal quarters of the Mai's palace where the princess lived. His mind wondered briefly into a speculative future where the sands of the Sahara had grown immensely and buried the city and with it all the secrets of the dead. Pensive and lost in thought, he was interrupted by the princess, "Abuyazid," she called. Startled, Bayajidda's eyes moved abruptly from the sand dunes beyond the oasis that he was blankly staring at back to the darkened room where his wife stood — frozen in shock.

"My love, Magira!" Shouted Bayajidda with an embracing gesture but the princess reclined and took a step back. His son came rushing into the room but after three years apart, the toddler could hardly recognise his father. "Who is this man," said the child.

"O, I am your father, little one." Bayajidda rose to his feet, disappointed at the princess for not telling the child about him. Anger was brewing inside him and like a raging tempest at sea, he opened his mouth to shout at the princess. He thought about all the things he would say to her and then force her to leave with him but he remembered the warnings of the giant. 'If he gets angry, the cloak will disappear and the Kenembu will know that he is not a Mai (king)'.

"Please leave, you are not welcome here," said Princess Magira.

"What has got into you?" asked Bayajidda but the princess was silent.

"Haha, you sneaky man," came a voice from the corridor leading to the princess' quarters. It was the Mai who had arrived with his entourage. "Clever trick. You have deceived the people with your little magical simulacrum but you cannot fool me. I know who you are," said the Mai (princess Magira's father).

"You old fool, I should have known you had something to do with this. What have you done to her?"

"Haha, haha. Accusations, accusations, that's all you know how to do. You were the one putting ideas into her head about her being queen, so that you can have a piece of this empire. Who ever heard of a woman being a leader? What is she going to do, lead you to defeat?" bantered the Mai (king) and his entire entourage laughed. Although to them, it appeared as simply two kings having a funny conversation. The king then turned around and headed back from the direction he came. "And make sure you leave my kingdom before nightfall, haha..." the Mai's voice trailed as he departed.

***

Sounds of footsteps awoke Bayajidda from a short cat-nap he had late in the afternoon and he realised that night had already crept and enveloped the oasis in total darkness. From beyond, desert winds wailed and brought with them chilled air. Light illuminated the hallway, growing brighter and brighter as the sounds of footsteps grew louder. It was Princess Magira standing with a candle. "You haven't left?" she asked, "and please close the window before we freeze," she added.

"What happened to your monarchical aspirations?" "Oh, so you'd be king? My father was right."

"No, he is not. It seems you are enchanted and I'll get to the bottom of it,"

"Just get out of here and please stay away. Just remember báràm, báràm, báràm."

~ 11 ~

JOURNEY TO ANCIENT GARAMA & THE BODÉLÉ DEPRESSION

"What happened in there? Did it work?" asked Nebu, as he sat strangely still on moving cattle. What strong back muscles he must have, thought Bayajidda. "Yes, the giant was right. I used the Ka-Nur symbol and the Ka-Mai and lo and behold, the Kenembu could not tell that I was in fact an outsider, haha," replied Bayajidda.

"What about Magira? I thought you'd rescue her from her evil father?" asked Nebu.

"No, she is safer there for now," responded Bayajidda. "What are you going to do?"

"I don't know, for now," replied Bayajidda, as they arrived at the ancient city of Garama which was irrigated by hundreds of underground aqueducts. A type of irrigation called qanat irrigation or *qanāh*. Once an empire of the Garamantes — a people who traded with the Romans, now just an extension of the Kenembu who referred to those areas all the way to the southern fringes of the expansive Sahel as the Borno. The whole area was once irrigated by the Great Lake Zad but now relied only on underground irrigation systems.

"The word *bahr-nuh* translates to 'sea of Noah'," commented Bayajidda.

"Interesting, Bayajidda but there is no sea here," replied Nebu, who seemed to be getting tired.

"You see only sand here now but over 600 years ago, the Great Lake Zad reached these lands," responded Bayajidda.

"Why did we travel North from Njimi?" asked Nebu with tired eyes and a long face.

"We are only passing through," replied Bayajidda.

***

As the sun reached its summit, Bayajidda stopped to take a rest at the shores of a river flowing south. While lying down comfortably on the ground, Bayajidda had a dream in which he saw darkness everywhere and a large snake laughing at him as it devoured an infant. He woke up with a start due to Nebu's screams. The sky had blackened by the worst 'sand-clouds' he had ever seen.

"Wow, we must take cover," shouted Nebu.

"The storm is coming from the Bodélé Depression. The very source of most of the dust in the world," shouted back Bayajidda as the clouds continued to form.

"There is a canoe, we must take it. The river looks very navigable and it is flowing south," said Nebu.

"Who told you I'm heading south, young man? I am

heading to the eye of the storm," barked Bayajidda.

"I am coming with you!"

"No, it is too dangerous. This is the only river flowing south from here. All others end up somewhere near the Bodélé Depression. I will see you back at the land of the Habe, my friend, if our paths be crossed again. Goodspeed!" Bayajidda bid young Nebu goodbye and headed north.

A lone hooded figure, wrapped by a long robe riding a camel deep into the uncharted desert while his companion Nebu, also alone and afraid, let fate guide him south.

~ 12 ~

THE SACRIFICE

Finally, after journeying for weeks, Bayajidda arrived at Bodélé Depression. Alone and with only his thoughts for company, he called out the ancient spirits which resided in the depression. "I yearn to find a solution," he said, as he performed an evocation. "Reveal yourself, The Triune. I call upon you!" As he repeated the phrase, he gradually developed a splitting headache — first in the front of his head, then the middle and then the back.

Within a few moments a woman stood in the middle of the dusty terrain. "What do you seek to know, traveller," she asked.

"I need to know how to get my army back from the Mai. They couldn't even recognise me when I went there. My wife fears me and my son does not know me. Tell me, spirit!"

"Haha, you dare come here with no offering and make demands?" replied the wraith, whose voice echoed from all directions. "I offer to you myself," replied Bayajidda, falling to his knees as he spoke those words. The spirit dematerialised and the storm seemed to have cleared momentarily but it formed again and the sky was as black as night. Huge clouds morphed into the face of a woman and it spoke, "It is I who rose when man was not. It is I who flies to all corners of the earth when man cannot. It is I who provides air for man to breathe and It is I who keeps the world intact. It is I who destroys and it I who fixes that which has been destroyed. It is I, the ancient one, the sustainer, the ever living, the glorious, the beautiful..." the clouds dispersed and the spirit took the form of a woman again, materialising behind Bayajidda who was still knelt down in the middle of the Bodélé Depression.

"...O Bayajidda I have accepted you as a sacrifice and I shall take you when the time is nigh. The world is bigger than one's ego, one's family and one's immediate sur-rounding. You must merge with me, O man! Begone now, and you will know what to do!"

~ 13 ~

ISKOKI (SCORCHING WINDS)

For three days Bayajidda could not see. He walked in total darkness across the barren, desolate and unforgiving landscape — as blind as a bat. The only thing that guided him was the voice of the Samuum-el; the spirit that now resided inside him. "My children will now guide you back to the land of the Habe and you will do our bidding. After that, your army who have been enchanted by the Mai's magicians will be released and they will bring your wife and child to you. Do not betray us Bayajidda or we will take you before the time eeeehhh- hhaaaa..." the wind whispered in Bayajidda's ears, as he walked alone, hearing no background noise, except the wailing of the wind. 'This way. No, turn to your right and keep going straight', the voice would say and sometimes when sleep overtook Bayajidda he felt the sensations of being lifted by the wind and a journey of a week shortened to a matter of hours.

Finally, with squinty eyes, Bayajidda awoke to the smell of wet soil. He rejoiced after looking around and seeing trees everywhere and he rejoiced even more because his vision had been restored by the Samuum-el and indeed he was no longer in the desert. He was lying down amidst a thick grove. Working his fingers, he felt the softness of fur beneath him and people about him.

"Are you okay?" said a young woman, trying to resuscitate Bayajidda.

"I'm okay, I'm okay," he replied, while getting to his feet. As he took a few steps, he realised that all the pain he had in his ankles had healed and he was feeling revitalised and refreshed, save for the sun burn he endured during his journey through the desert. "Where am I?" Bayajidda asked the young woman.

"You are in our home. We are the Azna people. We found you blindfolded and lying on the sand," she replied.

"Hmm, blindfolded," muttered Bayajidda.

"Yes, and there was a snake near you, but it got away when it saw us approaching," added the young woman. "Well, thank you, I must be on my way."

Bayajidda squeezed through hundreds of the Azna people who had gathered to see 'the man who was found on the ground'. Children, women and a few young men were itching to ask him questions. "What's your name?" asked a little boy but Bayajidda was concentrating on returning to the settlement where he had left his horse. "How do I get to a place they call Hadejia?" he asked randomly, his eyes moving from face to face in the crowd of Azna people. Finally, he glanced at a man who was standing alone at the edges of the grove where the trees became sparse. "You sir, perhaps you can help me?"

inquired Bayajidda but the man simply said, "Look behind you. Our Inna (mother) needs to talk to you." Turning around, Bayajidda saw the little boy who asked him what his name was. The child kept repeating the question again and again. "What is your name, sir?" he asked for the fifth or sixth time. Behind the little boy was an old woman about the age of sixty-five who smiled gently on meeting eyes with Bayajidda. "His name is Bayajidda," she said, "although that is strange, because the spirit of the ancient one flows through his veins. Bring him to my quarter."

Two powerful men grabbed Bayajidda's arms from behind, gripping him by his wrist firmly, such that he could not get away. For the first time in a few hours, Bayajidda heard the voice of the Samuum-el again whispering in his ears. "Remember, you must do our bidding."

***

Weeks later, Bayajidda remained with the Azna people, a sub clan of the Habe who had a matriarchal society and he had got familiar with quite a few of them and had also learned a lot from the Inna (mother) of the clan.

"You see everything has a spirit. The rocks, the trees and even a small grain of soil," the Inna said.

"I know, Inna," replied Bayajidda.

"I am sure you know. You are no ordinary man but the name they gave you does not sit too well with me," replied the Inna.

"Haha, it's just a name and it has a nice ring to it," responded Bayajidda.

~ 14 ~

'YA NA-JIDDA'

"I think you should change the name to 'ya na-Jidda', which means he does Jidda instead of 'he doesn't do' (ba ya) Jidda. Jidda being the religion of the old woman, as you know," said the Inna (mother). She laughed and made for the exit. While Bayajidda sat quietly, his mind far removed from the landscape. All he thought about was his wife and child and how his army would bring them to Habeland. Although as time went by, the promise made to him by the Samuum-el was becoming more and more like an illusory hope. In fact, he no longer heard the whispers of the spirit until one day, as he took a bath in a shallow pool, he heard the spirit say, "Be careful." Within a few seconds Bayajidda saw a large python swiftly gliding into the shallow pool and he attempted to go out but the snake wrapped itself on his left leg. Were it not for Nebu who hurled Bayajidda his sword, the snake would have got the better of Bayajiddah. As Bayajidda turned, the snake hissed and slid away while Bayajidda rushed out of the pool. "Nebu, my friend, thank you," said Bayajidda.

"No problem. What are you doing here with these witches?" asked Nebu.

"They are noble," replied Bayajidda

"But you must remember our ways," responded Nebu. "Yes, I know we are Christians from Baghdad and our ways are indeed different."

"I know they saved you but we must be on our way now, Bayajidda," said Nebu not knowing that a presence of unfathomable strength now compels his companion Bayajidda — the Samuum-el.

Bayajidda followed Nebu's lead toward the edges of the town but before leaving he was summoned by the Inna (mother), so, he headed back to the Inna's quarter while Nebu waited for him outside. "Please, before you go on your way, I need you to help the political leader of our clan. As you know I am the spiritual leader, the Inna (the mother) and the political leader or *sarauniya* (queen) is called Daurama. She is currently our *kabara* (leader). We have been having conflicts with another clan to the south. They blocked all our wells and now a powerful serpent guards our central well; our main source of water," said the Inna.

"What? A snake stops you from fetching water?"

"Yes, a serpent. It is my theory that the Dalawa (Kanawa/Kano) clan have found a way to infect our well," she replied. At that moment Bayajidda recalled what his wife was uttering when he was about to leave. It suddenly dawned on him that his wife had not lost her faculties at all and was in fact trying to protect their son. He remembered her words when she bid him goodbye in a manner he thought was severely cold at the time. He gazed blankly at the old woman while he tried to make sense of everything. His wife's words continued to play in his mind, 'Just get out of here and please stay away. Just remember *báràm, báràm, báràm.*' He recalled that his wife the Mai's daughter called their son Biram instead of Yazid but it was in fact a mispronunciation on his part. She was actually speaking in her native Kanembu language and *báràm* in that language meant 'a well'. Was she trying to tell him to go to the well? He wondered on and on.

~ 15 ~

TSUMBURBURAI (THE PHALLIC CULT)

"What did that old woman say? You look like you've seen a ghost, Bayajidda!" said Nebu.

"Oh, you have no idea. It's a long story. I'll tell you one day," replied Bayajidda as they walked out of the settlement of the Azna toward the south in the direction of the big city of Kano which citizens, according to the old lady were poisoning their wells. Bayajidda had nothing but admiration for the people that saved him and so he was determined to get to the bottom of it.

Humid winds with promises of rain blew on Bayajidda's face and he heard the Samuum-el whisper in his ear, "I am with you." Bayajidda felt reassured knowing that what he was on his way to do, constituted 'our bidding' as the spirit stressed he had to do. "I got your horse from the Habeland of Hadejia," said Nebu.

"Oh, my horse, Hisan," said Bayajidda, "thank you, Nebu."

Before long, they arrived at the city of Dala also called Kano. Bayajidda's imagination was captivated by the big city, named after its founders — a group of blacksmiths who called themselves Gana after the ancient Empire of Ghana known for mining gold. Those groups of people initially spoke Nupe language but have now been heavily influenced by Habe clans like the Azna whom they married. Bayajidda thought about the Aznas he stayed with for a few weeks and the political tensions they had with the Dalawa.

Before evening, Bayajidda reached the king's house and was welcomed with songs of praises. "To what do we owe your visit?" asked the king.

"I am here because the Azna and other clans have complained that their wells are being infested with snakes. Particularly, their central well and they are unable to fetch water," replied Bayajidda.

"That is a most strange thing. I don't know anything about that. I suggest you come with me to consult our priest at the Dalla Hill," replied the king of Dalla (Kano).

"Yes, your majesty, I shall come with you," agreed Bayajidda.

***

With a clenched fist Bayajidda took his first step outside the king's palace. Tall trees lined the way from the palace to Dala Hill where the chief priest resided. The road was narrow but long and on its sides were dancing girls and drumming boys. Captivated by the scenery but with some sense of urgency to the matter, Bayajidda asked, "How far is it, your majesty?" The king glanced at Bayajidda and noticed Bayajidda's unease, "What is the matter?" he asked.

"All is well, your majesty," replied Bayajidda, after sighting a large cuboid building at the base of the Dala Hill. "Oh, you must have thought we were going to climb the hill. Not at my age I can't climb the hill. You must be tired, haha," joked the king. That wasn't why Bayajidda was asking but he let the king have the laugh. "This is the place," commented Nebu to himself but loud enough for the King and Bayajidda to hear him.

The priest was a middle-aged man with a short rough beard, naturally formed dreadlocks and amulets all over his body. He pushed the door to the cuboid structure open, "Please walk inside, my king," he ordered. Curiously, he barricaded the door and stopped Bayajidda from accessing the temple. Surprised and a little ired, the king whispered to the priest, "That man is my guest. His name is Bayajidda, let him in." But the priest did not move from Bayajidda's path. Meanwhile the Samuum-el slightly materialising in the form of a small twister whispered in Bayajidda's ears, as the sounds of drums and singing continued in the background. "Look at the amulet around his neck," the spirit said.

Bayajidda looked away from the priest's eyes down to his neck and among the dozens of necklaces, there was a silver necklace adorned with a spiraling snake around a large emerald pendant. Not only was there a snake necklace around the priest's neck but statues of snakes everywhere in the temple too.

"Let them in, I said," the king repeated and Nebu walked straight through but the priest still stood right in front of Bayajidda — stopping him from going inside the cuboid temple. "This man is not who he says he is. *Ba ya Jidda?* More like *ya na Jidda!*" bellowed the priest. Sensing the presence of the Samuum-el in Bayajidda, the priest insisted that the visitor should not be allowed inside the cuboid temple at the base of the Dala Hill — the temple of Tsumburburai.

~ 16 ~

THE RETURN OF
BAYAJIDDA'S ARMY

Bayajidda returned to the Azna clan into a beautifully decorated hut provided to him by the Inna (mother) of the clan. The hut had three rooms and an outdoor sitting area like a parlour. It was made in preparation for when his family joined him. He leaned wearily against the wall — tired from all his quests. He rubbed his eyes with the back of his hands and gathered his thoughts. Outside, was sunny and the wind blew on branches of majestic trees creating a pleasant afternoon; perfect for a nap or perhaps an afternoon stroll but not for Bayajidda. He was going into a depressive state but before that could take hold; good news came. "Bayajidda, Bayajidda! People are coming," a small girl from the neighbourhood came rushing into Bayajiddah's compound to alert him about what was happening outside. "It looks like an exodus," commented Nebu who was staying at Bayajidda's house.

On stepping out, Bayajidda saw recognisable

faces among the crowd of military-looking individuals numbering nearly 4000. Bayajidda rushed toward them and they immediately bowed upon seeing their army general. "Get up, get up," he ordered, grabbing the face of a young soldier and pulling him up. "Where is Asur?" he asked.

"I am over here, Abuyazid! You live?" Asur was Bayajidda's second in command who they migrated from Baghdad together with, over six years ago. "And where is my wife and child?" a berserk Bayajidda asked, while he looked around fretfully at blank faces who appeared not to have any idea what he was talking about.

Meanwhile, black clouds darkened the afternoon to a near night ambience. Horrid winds blew and stirred up dust — a scene which would have caused emotional unrest in a different part of the world but in the middle of the savanna, though a freak weather, it was considered a blessing; an escape from the unending intensity of the sun. Bayajidda looked up at the sky as if to pray to God to help him find his wife but all he saw was the face of the Samuum-el, morphing inside the clouds and the spirit's voice in his ears. "I have done my part. I've liberated your army from the stranglehold of the Mai (king) of the Kenembu. Now complete our bidding, slay the serpent!"

"What about my family?" shouted Bayajidda.

"Haha, complete our bidding..." The Samuum-el's wicked innuendo carried on, as the clouds dispersed and the sun continued its ascent in a blaze of glory.

***

Moments later, an entourage pierced through the

crowd of Baghdadian soldiers, right to Bayajidda's hut. It was the Inna, the spiritual leader of the Azna in company of a group of armed men and the political leader of the Azna who was called Daurama, a woman of indescribable beauty but with no eyes for a man, for the *sarauniyas* (queens) of the Azna did not get married. She was helped down from her horse by a powerfully built young man and she walked straight to Bayajidda's hut and found him lamenting on the ground.

~ 17 ~

DAURAMA THE SARUNIYA/ QUEEN: POLITICAL LEADER OF THE AZNA

Bayajidda's hut was packed with onlookers among the Azna who had heard about their *sarauniya* (queen) but most had never seen her. All around the building were girls peering through windows; hoping to catch a glimpse of the elusive leader. They've heard so much about her iron fist, about her staunch demeanour and her air of confidence in dealing with the Dalawa and other warlike clans. Some have even heard myths that she was as strong as a male wrestler. Some boys mounted the walls around Bayajidda's compound while his second in command and a few of the Baghdadian soldiers walked into the compound — curious about what was happening.

Bayajidda was still crouched in a corner with his head down, saddened by the fact that his family were not among the army that had just arrived. He wondered if he would ever see them again. He felt the queen's piercing gaze on him as she stood by the door. "What is the meaning of all this? Our town is overrun by your soldiers. I demand an explanation!" she thundered. Indeed, she was just as her subjects have heard. She was fearless even though the Azna's were dwarfed by the presence of the Baghdadian soldiers — who had already set up watchtowers to help fortify the low-lying Azna homeland. Bayajidda had no idea what to say to the queen. He couldn't tell her why his army had come to the Azna homeland. He stood up with his back to the queen and walked out of the compound through the backdoor. He had just walked a few feet away from his hut when the queen commanded, "Bring him to the courts, he must answer to this recalcitrance!"

"Yes, our *Kabara* (leader)," answered one of her royal guards who then ordered four men to grab Bayajidda. Bayajidda heard the shuffling sounds of the men's footsteps behind him growing louder and louder and then the swoosh sound of Baghdadian swords being drawn from their sheaths. Within a second the Azna homeland was as quiet as cemetery; not a single person made a sound and then Bayajidda's voice broke the silence, "Let them take me," he said.

***

"You do not have to keep him shackled in chains," implored Asur, Bayajidda's second in command but the court macer carried on with his initial instructions ushering a chained Bayajidda to sit down on a wooden stool. Around the court was the clangour of drums and chants which came to a sudden halt as the judge stepped into the courtroom. "You will answer the question you've been asked," said Daurama, the queen of the Azna. She was seated on an elevated chair. Bayajidda, with his head still down and his arms bound, replied, "My army is here because they came with me from our home of Baghdad — a city farther than the great city of Meroe and across the Red Sea."

"It has come to my attention that you visited the Dalawa to confront them about the snakes they keep putting in our wells and in particular our central well, where there is a large snake inside. I don't know how they are doing it but the snake ins't there on Fridays. We can only fetch water on Fridays. What agreements have you come to?"

"Nothing, the priest denied me access to their temple but I saw snake statues inside. So, your theory could be right," replied Bayajidda. The queen did not look satisfied with Bayajidda's reply. "Take him to the old house, to learn!" she instructed.

***

The old house was at the town centre near the central well. Inside the house, Bayajidda saw statues and old scrolls. It was a historical repository for the Azna clan; housing their past. "The Dala people took over our town and desecrated our temple," said the queen, as Bayajidda was shown around — with his hands still bound by chains.

"The cuboid temple in Dala/Kano used to be yours?" "That is the truth," responded Daurama

For the first time Bayajidda looked at the queen right in her eyes and when their eyes met, the Samuum-el rushed out of Bayajidda's body and straight into the queen, "Now go to the well and whatever ophidian lurks there, slay it and you will have your family," shouted the Samuum-el, the spirit's voice coming from the queen's mouth. For a moment the queen massaged her throat, wondering why she sounded strange.

"So, they are here?"

"Go, now!"

~ 18 ~

THE SERPENT

As evening dawned, a beautiful purple tinged the sky and cold winds sighed through the rocky terrain making tumbleweeds rejoice as they rolled across. Onlookers numbering hundreds stood awestruck as the hero that he had come to be, walked from the old house to the well. What man dared enter the pit of the serpent? They must have wondered, but Bayajidda was no ordinary man.

With renewed vigour he walked on, turning around to see Asur his second in command, armed to the teeth, "I will come with you," he said.

"No, I must do this alone," replied Bayajidda. Nebu's eyes filled with tears after seeing his companion, general, and friend getting lowered into the well. The queen on the other hand was captivated by Bayajidda's gallant nature. Under the enchanting influences of the Samuum-el, all she could think about was the safety of Bayajidda; maybe she shouldn't have insisted that he went down there, she thought.

Inside the well, Bayajidda was met with a blackness he had never experienced — not even in the underground lake on the way to the Great Lake Zad. As he got to the bottom of the well, he lighted his torch — powered by cow bone marrow. The water inside the well was only ankle deep and retained the warmth of the day. For a moment Bayajidda chuckled to himself, no wonder they weren't getting any water, he thought. He looked around for a snake but there was nothing inside and particularly nothing big enough to stop anyone from fetching water but to his surprise a wall had caved-in, revealing a chamber. Without hesitation, he walked through and was met with an ancient underground habitation of some long-gone race.

Ancient statuary lined the edges of the chamber. Statues of snake veneration, and then he heard the unmistakable slithering sound of a snake; except there wasn't just one snake, there were several. None of the snakes attacked Bayajidda, most wanted to get away from the fire. He wondered if he should just go back up and seal the well but he was too curious. As he walked through the chamber, he heard a loud bang and a massive snake burrowed through the wall, stopping right in Bayajidda's face. "Oh, if it isn't Bayajidda himself," said the snake, "What have you come here to do, kill me? Ehahaha," added the snake.

"All I am here to do, is make you leave. The people can't fetch water because of you," replied Bayajidda.

"The people, the people, the people, the people. It's always about the people. Who cares about the people?" The snake slid from side to side, his large head only a few inches away from Bayajidda's face. The rest of the snake's body was still inside the tunnel and only half of it was outside. "Look, I'm only down here because of my family. If you leave their well, I get my family back. I'm sure there are countless wells you can go to," responded Bayajidda as he pulled out his sword. "Huh, I'm not afraid of your little sword, human, hahahaha. The Samuum-el used you. She is more of a danger to the town's people than me. You see, she used you as a vessel to get to the queen. She wanted to be in the queen all along ahahaha," explained the snake.

"I know that but my family come first,"

"Why did you have to summon her Abuyazid? Why?"
"I needed the help of something powerful, I had no
    choice," responded Bayajidda.

"But I have always been with you. Who do you think helped you survive throughout your adventures?" responded the snake, as he slid back and forth inside the chamber.

"What are you talking about? Stop being so nebulous!" Bayajidda took a swing at the serpent but the serpent dodged it and splashed water on Bayajidda — almost putting out the torch. "How can I stop being what I am? I have always been the nebulous one," answered the snake. He completely came out of the tunnel and towered over Bayajidda, "You puny man," he hissed.

"I am tired of your indirect talk! Go now or I'll strike you!"

"No!" responded the snake. Bayajidda then struck the snake with his sword and the snake became smaller. With every strike the snake shrunk and shrunk until it's head turned into a bloodied human head. Bayajidda could not believe his eyes, he mounted the torch on a side wall and went closer to the snake to observe the unnatural phenomena and the head spoke. "You dare strike down your friend?" It was the head of Nebu, Bayajidda's beloved companion. "How is this possible?" screamed Bayajidda and he began to cry uncontrollably. "You have failed again Abuyazid, you have failed again."

"Failed what, my dear Nebu? How are you the snake?" "No wonder you do not know your name. Life after

life, you fail. Abu Yazid is your *kunya* which identifies you through your child. Your personal name is your *ism* and your *laqab* is merely a nickname, which is what they call you here 'Bayajidda'. Your *nasab* is your clan name and finally your *nisab* is your place of birth. Tell me your name!"

"I don't know, I don't know," cowered Bayajidda in fear. "Are you Abu Yazid Makhlad ibn Kaydad the son of a Berber man and a slave girl called Sabika brought from

Europe and sold in the town of Tadmakat in Mali?"

"I don't know," repeated Bayajidda. With shaky legs, and stained with the blood of his dear friend-turned- serpent, Bayajidda staggered out of the chamber toward the well and called to be pulled up.

END

Ingram Content Group UK Ltd.
Milton Keynes UK
UKHW041342090723
424700UK00002BA/10